Mama Loves Me from Away

by **Pat Brisson**

Illustrated by **Laurie Caple**

Boyds Mills Press

*I am indebted to Warden Gladys Deese and Officer Brian Corbett of the
Julia Tutwiler Prison for Women in Wetumpka, Alabama, and to Carol
Potok from the service group, Aid to Inmate Mothers.
Special thanks to Morgan and Michele!*

—L. C.

Text copyright © 2004 by Pat Brisson
Illustrations copyright © 2004 by Laurie Caple
All rights reserved

Published by Boyds MIlls Press, Inc.
A Highlights Company
815 Church Street
Honesdale, Pennsylvania 18431
Printed in China
Visit our Web site at: www.boydsmillspress.com

Library of Congress Cataloging-in-Publication Data

Brisson, Pat.
Mama loves me from away / by Pat Brisson ; illustrated by Laurie Caple. — 1st ed.
32 p. : col. ill. ; cm.
Summary: When a mother and daughter are separated by the mother's
incarceration, they find a special way to keep their loving relationship alive.
ISBN 1-56397-966-7
1. Birthdays — Fiction — Juvenile literature. 2. Mothers and daughters —
Fiction — Juvenile literature. 3. Imprisonment — Fiction — Juvenile literature.
(1. Birthdays — Fiction. 2. Mothers and daughters — Fiction. 3. Imprisonment —
Fiction.) I. Caple, Laurie A. II. Title
[E] dc 22 PZ7.B7577Ma 2004

First edition, 2004
The text of this book is set in 14-point Stone Serif.
10 9 8 7 6 5 4 3 2

For Michael J. Tofani, M.D., whose work in forensic psychiatry
inspired me; and for all the parents and children who are forced by
circumstances to love each other "from away"

—P. B.

For the mothers at Tutwiler Prison, and everywhere,
who find ways to love their children from away

—L.C.

My BIRTHDAY is Mama's birthday, too.
"You're the best present I ever had," she always told me.
"Tell me again," I'd say.

So Mama told me how she was out at the club with her friend Sissy, celebrating Mama's nineteenth birthday. They were laughing and dancing when her pain started, the pain that meant I was on my way.

"Sugar, it hurt! But Sissy told me how I should
breathe and relax while she went to call Big Roger
to come in his truck and take us up to Saint Luke's."

"That's where I was born," I always tell Mama. And Mama, she pretends she hasn't heard that before.

"Is that a fact?" she always asks me with a smile.

I love hearing Mama tell the story.

"It was worth every minute of pain just to see you, Sugar, all slick and shiny, crying your little cry, your arms shaking with the effort. And from the first minute I saw you, I loved you. *She's mine*, I thought to myself. *She is my Sugar for all time*. You were the best birthday present ever!"

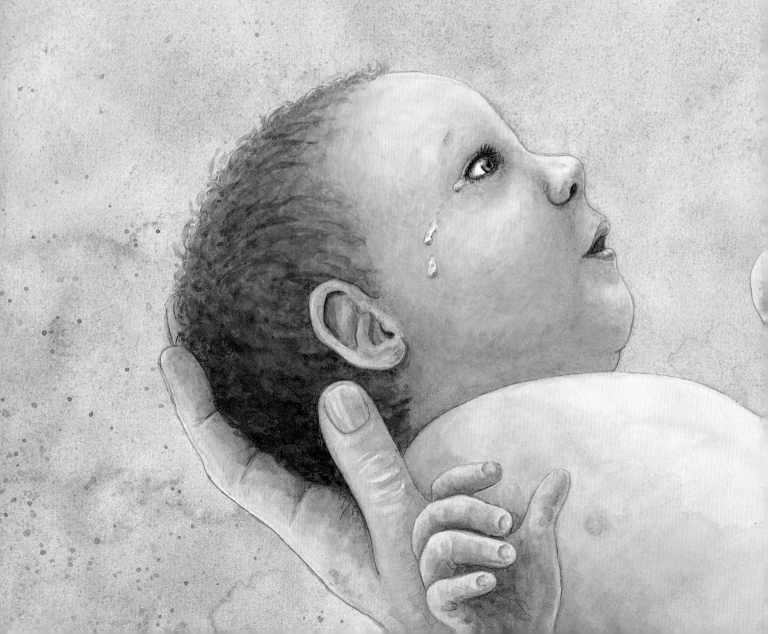

And when Mama told that story, I snuggled up next to her and listened with my ear against her chest. Then the words came, not through the air, but from Mama's heart right into my own. Mama told me lots of stories, but that is my favorite best one.

Every night before I went to bed, Mama told me a story. Sometimes it was about Mama and Big Roger and the time they went to the beach and Big Roger got bit by a crab. Sometimes it was about Mama and Sissy when they worked at a restaurant making pancakes and eggs over easy all through the night for truck drivers on their way to Florida or Kansas.

Sometimes it was about me when I was little and wandered off after a friendly dog, and Mama hollered herself hoarse looking everywhere for me.

Mama's stories were my favorite time of the day.
But then Mama went away, and everything changed.

Instead of Mama's stories, I got Grammy's stories, which just aren't the same. Grammy's stories are from too long ago about people I never met, but that wouldn't be so bad if I didn't miss Mama so much.

Mama will be away for a long time. We visit her on Sundays if Grammy's knees aren't acting up. It takes three long bus rides to get there.

Mama doesn't look the same without her red blouse and purple sweater and long, dangly earrings. Now she wears gray and looks like someone else until she smiles at me.

"When are you coming home, Mama?" I ask her every time.

"As soon as I can, Sugar, as soon as I can," she tells me.

But it's not soon enough and I miss her stories and her laughing. She holds me close and brushes my hair, but there are strangers all around, and it's not the same as home.

When our birthdays were coming, I drew Mama a birth-day card. On the front I wrote: "To the World's Best Mama from Her Sugar for All time," and inside I drew a picture. It was Mama dressed in a red dress with high heels and sparkly earrings. I drew me right next to her holding her hand. I put Big Roger and Sissy and Grammy there, too.

"Happy Birthday to US, Mama!" I wrote underneath.

Grammy said it was perfect and we would see Mama that Sunday "knees or no knees." I tried to picture Grammy without any knees. It wasn't hard, because she wears long dresses.

"But remember, Sugar," Grammy said, "your Mama won't have a present for you. There are no stores there for Mama to go shopping."

I knew there were no stores, but I couldn't imagine a birthday without a present from Mama. I tried to pretend it wouldn't matter, but it did.

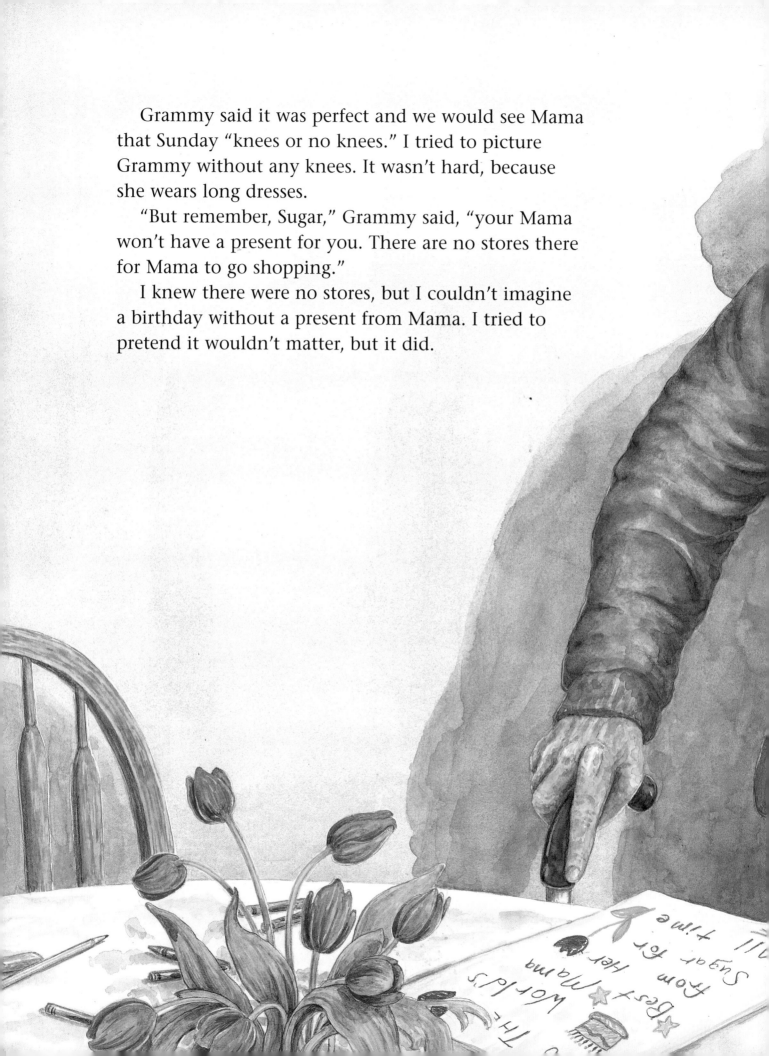

That Sunday, Grammy had good knees and we had no problems with the buses. I carried Mama's card extra carefully so it wouldn't get wrinkled. When we got there, Mama was waiting for us with a big smile on her face.

"Happy Birthday, Sugar!" she said, hugging me hard.

"Happy Birthday, Mama!" I said, hugging her and breathing in the smell of her hair and skin.

"You are getting so grown up!" Mama said. "I can hardly believe you were ever my tiny baby."

"But I was your baby, Mama, wasn't I? Tell me the story."

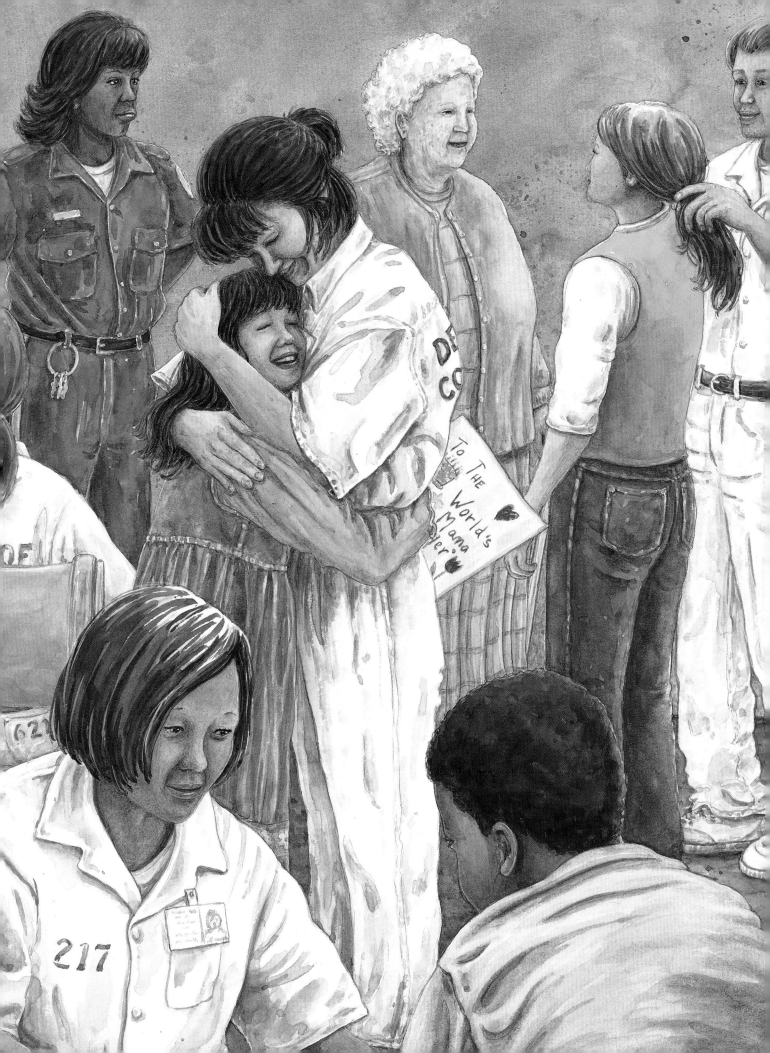

So she did. I closed my eyes and put my head against her chest and listened to the story straight from her heart just like I did when we were at home. And with my eyes closed, the strangers disappeared and I could pretend it was just Mama and me.

"I miss your stories, Mama. When are you coming home?"
"As soon as I can, Sugar, as soon as I can," she told me.
"But I have something for you that I think might help."
She took a notebook from behind the chair.
"Happy Birthday, Sugar," she said.

I opened the notebook. It was full of Mama's stories, and she had drawn pictures to go along with each one. There were seven stories, one for each day of the week: Sunday through Saturday.

"Here's the deal, Sugar," Mama said. "Every night at eight, you read the story for that day and I promise I will be here, whispering it to you through the night. Until I can be home with you again, Sugar, I will send you a story across the miles every night. It will be our special time."

I leaned against my Mama, my ear pressed to her chest. I held the stories close and brushed away two tears that wouldn't be held back.

Mama stroked my hair with her long, thin fingers and answered the unspoken question in my heart.

"As soon as I can, Sugar," she whispered, "as soon as I can."